WHEN THE SNOW FALLS

FIVE SHORT STORIES

DARA GIRARD

CONTENTS

ALSO BY DARA GIRARD

Collections

Domestic Disturbance (written as Dara Benton)

The Lady Next Door and Other Stories

Holiday Hearts

School Days: Five Story Collection

Lost and Found

Five Holiday Tales

10 Holiday Stories

Henson Series

Table for Two

Gaining Interest

Careless Rapture

Dangerous Curves

Familiar Stranger

Clifton Sisters

The Sapphire Pendant

The Amber Stone

The Emerald Ring

Novels

Honest Betrayal

The Daughters of Winston Barnett

Remember My Name

Illusive Flame

Winterwood Lane

Piece of Cake

This Changes Everything

INTRODUCTION

It's no secret that I enjoy writing short stories, especially those that can tie into a holiday. This collection blends some magical tales with other more down to earth ones, but all focus on taking a chance.

This collection starts with "Well-worn Dreams" a story set before Thanksgiving about a woman who prefers fantasy but must face the challenges of her present life.

In the fantasy story "Silence" a boy makes a wish for Christmas that comes true in an unexpected way.

In "For All Time," another story tinged with fantasy, a woman who prides herself on planning everything must now plan on learning to let go.

In "One Snowy Night," a child who loves snow enjoys a magical encounter with it and someone else.

And finally in "The List" a young man makes a decision to help an older man and ends up changing both of their lives forever.

I hope you'll enjoy reading this collection of holiday stories as much as I did writing them.

Dara Girard

December 2022

WELL-WORN DREAMS

WELL-WORN DREAMS

Fantasies were much better than real life.

Reality was messy, mostly sad and, for Candice, mostly miserable. But in her fantasies everything was perfect. Like right now. At this perfectly delicious moment in the library, watching Conner Yardley take notes, by hand, on a large yellow writing pad, she imagined him writing a love letter to her. And at any moment he would look up at her and smile. A slow, sexy smile that always made her feel weak in the knees.

She didn't know the real name of the man taking notes from a large book titled *Integrative Oncology* resting on the round table (she'd seen the cover of the book before he'd taken a seat), but that didn't matter. The name "Conner" suited him. Conner was perfect. She'd given him that name because she thought the consonants and vowels complemented the sound of her name. Candice. Candice Adams and Conner Yardley sounded like a perfect pair.

Of course her real surname wasn't "Adams", it was Mbionwu, but in her fantasy her surname was simple and Anglo. Easy to say and definitely easy to remember. Just like Conner.

Candice turned a page in the sleek travel magazine she wasn't reading, making sure not to stare. She'd been fantasizing about Conner for four months now ever since she'd first spotted him in the health section (he'd picked up a book on healthy eating). He'd walked past her and smelled like spring—fresh and new. Clean as a blank slate. Most of the men at the small, one level library were heavy with baggage: Either kids, youth (i.e. high school students) or hygiene (meaning they didn't have any), although the library didn't have too many homeless patrons since the county had opened up a community center down the road.

But Conner was just what her imagination needed. Candice turned another page of her magazine and sighed as she stole another glance at him. She sat one table away from him. At first it had been three, but after twice having her view obstructed by others—a group of students studying and then a lean looking man with East African features learning English with his tutor (a well meaning middle aged woman with a southern accent)—she made sure her view wouldn't be obstructed again. He came every Tuesday and Thursday at 4PM. Watching him was fun and she'd tucked every aspect of him into memory. He was in his mid to late thirties, of medium height, with almond brown skin, dark brows and lashes, and striking, handsome features.

He worked as an oncologist at the local hospital (she'd given him this profession since he was always reading books on pathology and seemed particularly interested in both oncology and immunology). He lived in a detached house just on the cusp of the exclusive Red Creek neighborhood and owned a dog, a mixed breed, which he'd rescued from a shelter two years ago after a breakup with his last girlfriend who didn't understand him like Candice did (he always liked to remind her how much). He took his coffee with almond based cream because he was lactose intolerant; he spoke three languages but only two very well and was trying to master the third. He liked bike rides, fly-fishing, hiking and hang gliding. He had taken classes through the Maryland school of Hang Gliding and become addicted, enjoying the hobby both in the state and in Hawaii. As much as he loved the sky he also loved the ocean and had seen the Great Barrier Reef. He took amazing photographs, which he liked to send to her. He was close to his family, particularly his mother and brother, who was three years his junior. They were both the eldest in their families.

Conner fit easily into her life. There were no arguments or fights. He was always patient and understanding with her and abhorred chaos as much as she did. Candice glanced down at the travel magazine and smiled at the picture. It was a full color spread of a beach off the coast of Morocco. That would be their next destination. She'd plan everything (they'd already travelled to

Portugal, South Africa and New Zealand) and he always let her because he trusted her decision.

Candice bit her lip and sighed, wistful. It was nice to have someone trust her. She liked a well ordered life, although others teased her about it and even hinted that she might be a little obsessive. But they didn't understand. Growing up with a mother who was generous with her love, but low on sense forced Candice to endure a life she couldn't control. A life she'd hated.

She'd lived in twelve different apartments, four different states, and two countries before the age of thirteen. Her mother was scatter-brained about almost everything—misplacing or forgetting things, from where she'd placed her glasses to her bills to the name of Candice's birth father (it seemed to change every year). She'd once left Candice's younger sister, Anna, fast asleep in the bread aisle of the grocery store. Fortunately, Candice had realized her mother's mistake before Anna woke up alone in the shopping cart. (That memorable summer afternoon she'd waited inside the car for them to come back and noticed something was missing when her mother arrived with food laden bags and no sister). At nine years old, Candice decided to do the shopping after that and continued even after her mother finally married a man who kept them from moving.

Twenty-three years later, Candice tried her best to keep her distance (her mother lived in South Carolina, she lived in Maryland) although her mother begged to see her once a year at the annoying US holiday people called Thanksgiving. Candice did her best to avoid it and had managed to do so for the past five years, telling her mother she had work, or a cold, or travel, or something.

She didn't only stay away because she knew her mother would overcook some aspect of the meal or her stepfather would tease her about how she polished every utensil before she used it but because she also had to deal with her two younger sisters. Her sister, Anna, was broke, unemployed and still living with their parents but because she was pretty, charming and clever her life seemed more tragic than pathetic. Candice's youngest sister, Brooke (the one who never had to worry about moving or being left in a shopping cart) was the pride of their parents' eye and every holiday made it her mission—having given up on Anna —to pepper Candice with questions about her long term goals and ambitions (at nineteen she'd already achieved four of hers, including getting into MIT, publishing a book, developing a software that provides a collaborative platform for brainstorming and task management for organizations, and dating a Rhodes scholar.)

Candice was proud of her youngest sister and, in turn, found her own life a source of embarrassment. Her well-planned life hadn't turned out the way she'd hoped. No matter how much she'd studied, she hadn't gotten into Wellesley College, the university of her literary idols: Angelina Weld Grimke, Judith Martin and Nora Ephron. Instead, she'd ended up attending a little no name school in Delaware. She'd had visions of becoming a distinguished English professor and Senior Lecturer, and becoming a member of the Modern Language Association and the International Society for History of Rhetoric.

But, instead, she didn't make it to graduate school because her mother got sick and needed someone to look after her, while her stepfather continued to work and her younger sisters lived their lives (Anna was useless in a crisis and Brooke had been too young). Thankfully, her mother recovered, but Candice's precise three year plan had been sidelined. She ended up writing ad copy for a college friend of Anna's who was starting a beauty line in Baltimore. They liked her work and eventually offered her a job. She would have turned them down if she hadn't been desperate for work (writing about color schemes and the consumer habits of various demographics was a far cry from the academic analysis of the best use of magniloquence). After a few months, she ended up as a marketing researcher helping the company expand.

However, after two years, she hadn't gotten the promotion she'd targeted. She'd actually lost the promotion to a Wellesley graduate (argh!), and due to a company takeover, she'd eventually lost her position (a position she'd never imagined having in the first place) when her job was made redundant (double argh!), which, after a fruitless ten month job search (no one seemed to know quite what to do with her), she'd been forced to start her own company. A consulting business that sprang from the simple, pointed, but instructional blog posts she'd started after her lost promotion several years before.

She'd written the blog hoping to prove that she was beneficial to the company. She'd crafted essays about the language of marketing, helping business owners and freelance writers understand terms used and how to spot authentic ways to connect to their target audience. The blog grew, as did a subscription base and people wanting to use her services. The business had been in existence for two years and paid the bills but was nothing to brag about, yet. She'd started coming to the library with the thought of returning to school, getting her PhD and entering the academic life of which she'd once dreamed.

She liked to hide in the library to get out of her house and to break away from the long hours of work—getting new clients while satisfying the few clients she had, while also researching and keeping up the weekly blog and completing all the administrative parts of the business, which took up most of her time. She dreamed of the day she could afford a part time assistant.

The library was always a place she enjoyed for the knowledge. She liked to know as much as she could. Especially the name of obscure things such as the name for the metal or plastic end of a shoestring (an *aglet*) to the name of the panicky feeling you get just when you're about to introduce someone whose name you can't remember, (*tartle*, from the Scots). She tried to learn a new word every day. Names gave things order. Gave some meaning to her life.

Just like Conner Yardley.

She looked at him and imagined that that morning they'd had their typical oatmeal breakfast together, topped with banana and raspberries drizzled with honey. She preferred sugar, but liked to watch the slow, specific way he let the sweet, golden liquid sweep over the fruit.

The Japanese word, *koi no yokan*, meaning the sense upon first meeting a person that the two of you are going to fall in love, suddenly came to her. She liked the word but didn't believe it. She was pleased that she'd never been in love; never gotten her heart broken. That kind of messiness was reserved for others. She was different and took no shame in it. In her fantasies it didn't matter that she didn't kill spiders or flies, that she had a different toothbrush for each day of the week, that her pantry was organized by size and color, that she didn't like to be touched (her mother's hugs always made her cringe) or that people, as a whole, were a complete mystery to her. She could sell to them (the psychology of language made sense) and help them on a purely intellectual level, but kept her distance for fear she'd be revealed as a fraud.

But in her fantasies that was never a problem. There was no fear of rejection or suspicion. She was always accepted. She wasn't the shy new kid who others whispered about and called weird. She wasn't the work colleague people didn't invite for after work drinks. She wasn't the daughter who had to lie to her family so she wouldn't have to see them at Thanksgiving.

Candice began to practice in her head what this year's excuse would be—a new, important client wanted her to deliver a project in three days—when she saw Conner get up and put on his sable colored coat. She glanced at her watch alarmed. He wasn't supposed to leave yet. Why was he leaving so soon? She took a deep breath. She had to relax. There must be a reason. Of course there was a reason, she chided herself. He was a successful oncologist who lectured around the country. Perhaps there was an urgent matter to deal with at the hospital. He was very conscientious and his supervisor had recently given him more responsibility, so he was eager to prove himself. Candice began to expand on her fantasy as she watched him put the books on a rolling cart, for the librarian to return to the shelves, and head for the door. She blinked when she noticed a square yellow envelope fall out of his black backpack.

Her heart froze. That wasn't supposed to happen either. He wasn't supposed to leave anything behind. This wasn't good.

She swallowed, her heart racing, her skin feeling hot. Should she tell him? No, she didn't want to talk to him. That would ruin everything. *Absolutely everything!* It was bad enough he was already ruining the pattern she'd created for them. She glanced at the yellow envelope on the purple carpeted floor. What if it was something important and he left and went to work and discovered it was lost and didn't know where he'd lost it? What if he searched all over his car and house wondering where he'd left it and in his distress he drove erratically around town, searching his mind, trying to retrace his steps to figure out where he could have left it and in his distraction he sped through a red light and got hit by a semi-truck?

He was almost to the door. Maybe he'd take a minute and turn around. Candice licked her lips and watched him, waiting, hoping, but he never looked back.

Maybe someone else would see it and tell him. Candice frantically looked around wishing the woman at the copy machine or the woman at a free standing shelf with library books for sale, would look at the ground, but they didn't. No one else seemed to notice the object on the floor. She realized that even if someone finally did notice it, they wouldn't know to whom it belonged.

She squeezed her eyes shut. This wasn't happening. She'd imagined it all. When she opened her eyes the envelope would be gone and she could go back to pretending again. Maybe someone would pick it up and throw it away. That's it! If it was thrown away then it wouldn't be her problem anymore.

She took a deep breath and kept her eyes closed. If it was still there she would do something, if not she'd forget it. She opened her eyes.

It was still there.

She swore.

She snatched up the envelope and raced out the library. She immediately felt the cold November chill against her cheeks, though her cashmere blouse kept her from completely feeling uncomfortable. She chewed her lip as her gaze scanned the parking lot. Fortunately it wasn't a large lot, barely five rows deep, and she soon spotted Conner walking to a beat up looking dark colored Honda. Her heart sank. He was supposed to drive a Lexus. She mentally shook her head. That didn't matter. She'd give him the envelope then return back to the warm library and the beauty of her dreams.

"You dropped this," Candice said, waving the envelope at him as if it threatened to fly out of her hands.

He stopped, halfway between getting inside his car, and looked at her, startled. She looked away. She didn't want to meet his eyes; she didn't want him to notice her. She knew he would think she was weird and that would ruin everything. She'd worked months on their fantasy together and she didn't want reality to intrude. She waved the envelope at him with more urgency. "Here."

She felt him take it, slowly. "Thanks," he said. "I—"

She didn't care. She didn't want to talk to him. She didn't want him talking to her. She wanted to be invisible. She turned and ran back inside the library, hoping he wasn't watching.

"Why did you run away?"

Candice kept her gaze on the elegant looking couple dining at a mountain resort in the travel magazine laid out in front of her.

Conner was talking to her. He'd followed her into the library, taken a seat at her table and started *talking* to her. It was her worst nightmare. He wasn't supposed to do that. At least his voice matched her fantasy. He had a low well modulated tone, although she detected a hint of an accent she couldn't place yet, but she'd make it up later. When he left her alone.

He held out his hand. "Kirwan."

She felt like crying. He was ruining everything. She didn't want to know his real name. Ugh and *Kirwan*? Kirwan and Candice sounded awful together.

She briefly shook his hand then gripped her hands under the table, keeping her gaze lowered. "Candice."

She heard the chair move across the carpet in a soft whisper as he settled into his seat. "Candice, you're a life saver."

His accent sounded slightly French. Maybe he was an immigrant from Belgium...no the French West Indies who...

"That letter you gave me was from my sister."

...had grown up here when his parents settled into the area when he was twelve.

"We haven't spoken in a while."

Argh! Why was he telling her this? This was none of her business. She nodded, hoping that would be enough of an acknowledgement for him to thank her again and leave.

The yellow envelope slid in front of her.

"Read it."

Her head shot up. She stared at him alarmed. "What?"

He nodded to the envelope. "Read it. Please."

She glared at the envelope wanting to rip it into shreds. It had ruined everything. Why would he ask her to read it? Was he illiterate? No, she knew that wasn't the case. She'd seen him writing copious notes. She knew he could read and write and spoke three languages! No, wait, she'd made that up. Argh! Bloody hell! Damn! Why was he doing this to her? Was this some sort of cruel joke?

He clasped his hands together and rested his elbows on the table, his tone intense. "I know it's a lot to ask and I know it sounds strange, but I've been carrying that letter around for two months without the courage to open it. Sometimes bad news sounds better coming from a stranger."

She tapped the side of the table with her thumb and met his gaze. He still had a nice face—she'd never seen him this close up—although his eyes were too serious. "Bad news rarely comes in a card."

"You'd be surprised."

Yes, she would, but then she rarely received cards.

"Please."

Candice took a deep breath. Conner wasn't suppose to have a sister, especially not a sister he hadn't spoken to in awhile. Her Conner came from a tight knit family, a loving home. She'd had a meal with them where they'd prepared...

She took a deep breath. This was reality. She'd do this one thing for him and then that would be that. He would go back to where he belonged, the stranger one table from the right with the sable colored jacket and large black watch.

Candice carefully opened the envelope dand pulled out the card. It had a picture of a sunset and two people in silhouette sitting on a grassy hill. She sent him a look of warning. "Are you sure you want—?"

"Yes," he said both his tone and gaze resolute.

Candice nodded and began to read. "*Dear Kirwan, I read your letter and I know what you want from me, but I'm not ready to forgive you yet...*" Candice faltered. This was even worse than she could have imagined.

He leaned back and rested his palms on the table. "Go on."

"*You hurt us all for so long that I can't trust that you won't hurt us again. I know you said you've changed, but I'm afraid to believe that. I'm glad you're well, but please leave me in peace until I can stand to see your face again. Lauren.*"

Candice replaced the card and slid it back to him.

"Thanks."

"I'm sorry," Candice said not knowing what else to say. She knew there was a word for a moment like this but it had escaped her mind.

Kirwan shook his head. "Don't be." He tucked the envelope in his backpack. "I knew there was a reason I didn't read it. I got exactly what I deserved." She could tell by the expression on his face, the hungry sadness in his eyes that he wanted to share his story. Part of her wanted to stop him. Part of her wanted to save what little she had left of the fantasy life she'd created for them. But with one encouraging nod she gave him permission to completely shatter it.

He folded his arms. "All my life I dreamed of being a success. I worked my way into building a lucrative rehabilitation and wellness center that I turned into a franchise. I made a lot of money and bought my parents a new house, new cars. I wore the best clothes, mingled with other top movers and shakers and I had plans for the next ten years. Then I started feeling tired, exhausted, but I ignored it."

He leaned forward and lowered his voice, forcing Candice to lean in too. "I started losing weight, I ignored that too, but I couldn't ignore the nagging cough." He ran a hand down his face and sighed like a world weary solider. "Non-Hodgkin's Lymphoma brought me to my knees. I got an aggressive strain that stole nearly everything from me. I lost my business because I was too arrogant and short-sighted to build a company that could run without me. I took pride in all that I did and I didn't delegate, so when I got sick it crumbled like a sandcastle in a storm.

"And, as my business failed, so did my finances and the medical costs reached their max and forced me into bankruptcy." He lowered his gaze and gripped his hand into a fist. "But I fought to survive. I did all I could to make it." He released his grip. "And in the end I knew that I was just lucky. Because along the way, doing my treatments, I met others who were stronger than me, kinder than me, more deserving than me who didn't make it. But I did." He lifted his dark gaze to hers. "And learned that nobody cared. Nobody cared if I lived or died. No, don't shake your head. I mean nobody. I'm not exaggerating.

"I hadn't realized who I'd become on my way to the top. How I'd isolated myself from everyone else. How ruthless and insensitive I'd been. I'd pushed away the very people who were supposed to love me because they didn't serve my purpose. It was only after getting sick that I realized how empty that purpose was. I changed. For the past year I've turned my back on my old life and worked towards redemption. One of the tasks I'd given myself was to write to the people I'd hurt the most and ask for forgiveness." He flashed a sad smile. "As you can see, that's not going to be easy."

"Have you gotten other replies?"

He opened his backpack and set two unopened envelopes on the table then pulled out his cell phone and showed her two unread messages.

She took a deep breath. "How many did you send out?"

"Ten." He pointed to a green colored envelope. "That's from my parents."

She swallowed then reached for it.

He covered her hand. "No, not yet."

She nodded. She understood. He'd had enough bad news for one day. "Are you okay now?"

He put the cards and cell phone away. "I'm in remission." He flashed a sad smile. "When I got sick, I realized I'd built an empty life and I'm not sure I'll ever miss that life again, but this new life is lonely." He looked around the library. "I come here because I have another idea for a wellness center that helps those going through medical challenges, similar to the ones I faced, not to feel alone."

She now understood all the books he had been reading.

She realized they were both looking for something

that wasn't there, hidden in the books: A cure for loneliness.

He'd made his dream come true and she'd lived in her mind, but they were both false. They had no true basis in reality and he'd learned a painful lesson that success won't always make you happy. They'd both had their fantasies shattered. For him it was one he'd built and for her it was one she'd created.

She met his gaze seeing a man who'd been a jerk, maybe worse, who wanted to change, who needed a second chance and she liked him, which scared her a little. "I've failed at everything I've tried," Candice said, her voice cracking a little with pain. "College admission, job search, promotion, even the business I have now isn't where I want it to be." She waited for the judgment, the smirk of derision, but it didn't come.

She now felt ashamed of all her petty grievances. So her business wasn't a booming success, at least she enjoyed what she was doing. So what if her title wasn't as esteemed as being an English professor? Yes, her mother could drive her crazy, but she could depend on her love. Anna could be reckless, but at least she had a stepfather to keep her in line and Candice had always liked him. Her brilliant sister Brooke worried about her, but that meant she cared. She wasn't alone. She did have a family, people who would miss her if she were gone. She and Connor, no Kirwan, had both been dreamers. It was time to wake up.

"W-would you like to spend Thanksgiving with me...uh...us?"

He stared at her stunned. "Your husband wouldn't mind a strange man coming to—?"

"No, I'm not married. You'd be meeting my mom, stepfather and two sisters."

"I'd like that. Thanks." He cleared his throat. "I'd always wanted to get a chance to know you better."

She blinked. "Me? Really?"

He nodded. "You always looked so happy in your own little world and I wondered how you did it."

She rubbed her hands under the table, feeling her cheeks burn. She liked him a lot and feared it would be ruined, but as she saw the soft smile on his face and the genuine joy in his brown eyes she let her fears subside a little. She'd enjoy the moment right now. A beautiful, heady moment she didn't have to make up. It was real. It was true. It was golden.

"I'll read the other cards and messages for you when you're ready."

Kirwan glanced at his watch, bit his lip, hesitated then said, "How about tonight? Coffee or dinner? It's up to you."

"How about both?" Candice said, feeling slightly reckless. "One for each card?" She knew there could be pain and disappointment, but she wasn't afraid.

He stood, looking equally unafraid. "Sounds good. I know a place to get coffee that's a couple blocks from here. I could drive or we could walk there...unless you have other plans."

She did. She had a schedule. She had every hour organized. "A walk would be nice."

He smiled and they gathered their things then headed to the exit. He held the door open for her and she tugged on the collar of her coat, shielding her against the brisk air.

"Is it too soon to hold hands?" he asked.

She shook her head then took his hand, pulled a face and kissed it, making him laugh.

She smiled, glad he no longer felt alone and neither did she. Fantasies may be perfect, but sometimes real life was so much better.

SILENCE

SILENCE

If he put his hands over his ears and closed his eyes maybe Christmas wouldn't come and they'd stop shouting. Damion Herold sat inside his bedroom closet among the smell of cedar balls and old leather, making himself as small as he could. He felt the hardwood floor beneath him, the cool wall against his back, wishing he could melt into it.

The shouting penetrated everything. The walls, the closed doors to both his bedroom and the closet. It seemed to seep into every crevice and crack—there was nowhere to hide. He'd once tried staying in the bathroom and running water in the sink and bathtub, but that didn't help. Neither did earplugs or earmuffs. Music blasting through headphones should have helped, it seemed to help everyone else, but not him. The shouting was too strong. It was like a colorful wave wrapped in vibration that he could see and feel. And every year he could see its pattern more clearly.

The shouting always grew worse in October just around the time the pumpkins started to show their funny or grizzly faces on doorsteps and the leaves began to change. It got worse in November, especially before Thanksgiving when family came to visit, although his parents were careful never to argue in front of them. He'd learned to associate the scent of hot rolls and turkey stuffing with the simmering argument that would erupt when everyone left. He once asked his grandfather and aunt to stay longer and they'd just smiled and patted him on the head, telling him he was a "sweet boy" and promising they'd see him next year.

But he wasn't trying to be sweet. He was scared. And he didn't like to be left alone with the shouting.

By December the shouting was like the deafening roar of a waterfall, but without the beauty. He remembered a trip to Niagara Falls once and was amazed by its power. Right now he felt as if he could be drowned by sound as its visible and vibratory power shot through the house like waves as high as towers before they crashed down to the floor in shades of red, green and blue. Sometimes they seemed to punch holes in the walls, but no one else seemed to notice.

No matter how good he tried to be, his parents always found a reason to be angry.

They reminded him of the robotic death matches his cousin Sara once took him to when her university was in the top finals. He'd seen the metal arms of their robot enter the cage and destroy the competitor, only to be defeated by another robot with an even swifter killer blow.

That robot reminded him most of his dad. He seemed angrier ever since he came back three years ago after being gone for a year. Nobody would tell Damion or his brother, Charlie, where their father had been. Damion knew his father wasn't a solider (he was no hero like his friend Kirk's dad who got a huge welcome from the whole town when he finally recovered after losing a leg and definitely not like his Aunt Nadine who came back from the Persian Gulf "funny in the head", whatever that meant).

The year his father had been gone felt like forever. He'd left when Damion was five and Charlie was three. His mom said it was for work and Damion imagined his father travelled a lot but wondered why he never wrote or called. He missed the smell of steam and the hissing sound of the iron as his father pressed his shirts every weekend. He longed for the scent of coffee in the morning and orange juice. He knew his father worked in an office, but not much else. When his father was gone, his mother always complained about money. When Damion finally asked her why Dad wasn't giving her any money, she told him he wouldn't understand. At first he thought she missed him. She was always saying under her breath "I wish Terence was here" and now he was and things weren't any better.

There was no smell of the iron or coffee just beer and ginger ale, plus the fruity scented drink that his mother sipped throughout the day. She seemed to sip a lot of it during the holiday season, but then people seemed to drink more when it got cold. "Keeps your body warm so the fairies won't get you," his grandfather had once told him in his deep island lilt when he'd let him have a sip of rum before his mother scolded them.

But Damion didn't worry about being cold or the fairies. He'd stopped believing they'd come and swallow him up long ago. He didn't care about the darkness coming sooner at the end of the day. He didn't like the coming holidays, and winter, because there was nowhere to escape. Sometimes he could escape in his dreams, where a beautiful woman with large brown eyes and a soft voice kept the sounds away and made him feel safe. In the spring and summer he could stay outside as long as he wanted—away from all the painful sounds—but not in the fall and winter.

Winter meant Christmas. The shouting was always the worse then.

Christmas was supposed to be a happy time, but he dreaded it. He dreaded the gifts that would come. Lots of gifts.

Gifts he stuffed in his closet and under his bed. Some he gave away (remembering that his grandmother always told him it was better to give than to receive), others he sold (because his mother always told him that money was important and only fools thought otherwise). His parents didn't notice the disappearing gifts or the extra cash that ended up in their wallets. Twice they caught him putting it there, but they didn't ask questions. They never asked questions. They never noticed anything he did.

They barely noticed he was around.

They didn't even look at him. He felt invisible.

At school he had friends, people said his name, but at home, nobody cared. Nobody cared how his day had been. His homework was looked over by the tutor. His parents never had time.

But they had time to shout at each other. And they'd take a minute to ask him what he wanted for Christmas.

That seemed to be the only time they listened to him.

And this Christmas he really wanted them to.

"WHAT DO you want for Christmas, Damion?" his mother asked as she stacked the dishwasher. He inwardly winced as he watched her, knowing his father would tell her she was stacking it wrong. Damion sent a nervous look at the kitchen entrance hoping his father wouldn't come in, then he caught sight of his brother shaking his head. Damion had told Charlie what he was going to ask for but Charlie had said it wouldn't work. But his brother was young and he was always putting his ideas down. The shouting didn't bother him as much. He never had trouble falling asleep and could watch a show with the volume turned high and not be bothered. Even as a baby nothing startled him.

Damion was different. Everyone in the family thought so, but couldn't say why.

He sighed and looked at his mother. "Just for one

day..." He swallowed hard. "I don't want you and Dad to fight."

She set the plate down on the counter. "What else do you want?"

"That's it."

She slammed the dishwasher closed, causing him to jump as he saw a beam of red sound crash against the wall. "Why are you asking me this?" She rested a hand on her hip and glared at him. "Do you think the fights are my fault?"

He watched his brother scuttle quickly out of the room before he said, "No."

Her tone sharpened, her dark eyes nearly as black as her braided black hair. "You think I want us to live like this?"

"Mom, I didn't mean."

His father stormed into the room, wearing a grey sweatshirt that made him look bigger than he was. "What's going on here? What was that bang?"

"Your son thinks I'm the reason we argue."

Damion shook his head. "I didn't say that." He sighed, hanging his head. "Never mind."

"But what was that bang?" his father asked.

Damion lifted his head ready to accept the blame, but his mother spoke before he could. "The dishwasher door," she said.

His brows shot up. "Are you trying to break it?"

"Did you even hear what I just said?"

"Do you know how much a replacement would cost?

You should know. You're the one always bitching about money."

"If you made any..."

"I make enough. You just spend all of it."

"If you hadn't..."

Damion didn't stay to hear the rest. He covered his ears and raced out of the room. The argument lasted the rest of the night into the following evening. He regreted saying anything. He hid in his closet, closed his eyes and held his hands over his ears and wished hard. The ground seemed to glow with the power of their anger, sound dripping from the ceilings, clinging to the walls. He wished for silence. *Silence. Please.* All he wanted was the shouting to stop. The tears to stop. Just perfect silence.

A sound, it looked like a fireball, shook the house, followed by another that pierced his heart with a cold chill. Before he could move, another sound rang out filling every crevice with a bright light before it quickly turned to black...then silence.

Perfect silence.

Perfect eerie silence.

A silence that would haunt him for years.

THAT NIGHT he remembered the smell of gunpowder, the scratchy feel of his neighbor's wool coat against his cheek, as she shielded him from the sight in the living room, the bright blue and red lights swirling in the darkness outside as people watched the chaos around his house. He remembered the questions and the sight of Charlie shivering in the back of an ambulance, barefoot, wearing his favorite red and black polka dot pajamas. They locked eyes and Damion felt the accusation in his brother's eyes. *This is your fault.*

Damion quickly looked away and stared at the house across the street where bright green lights danced across the surface while a large statue of a tiptoeing Santa stood on the roof.

HE NEVER CRAVED SILENCE AGAIN.

He lived in the cocoon of noise.

Every moment was filled with noise. He made sure to always have music, podcast or a show as a background diversion. Silence scared him. He knew it brought death.

He also learned to shout. He felt more alive when he shouted. More in control. His voice could keep silence away. That's how he hated and loved. That's how he dealt with discovering why his father had disappeared for a year (he'd been in prison after embezzling funds from his company, through his charm and a great lawyer he'd served barely a third of his sentence); how he'd handled the truth of the night his parents left him (his mother had gotten angry after one too many of her fruity drinks and shot his father before killing herself. No one ever knew what the argument had been about, but could only speculate). He used his booming voice to handle everything. When he turned twenty-nine his black hair turned silver white and he met a woman who loved to shout too.

Until she didn't.

Until she told him that she was tired of shouting; that she didn't want to be angry anymore. He didn't understand her. He wasn't angry. He was just being himself, dealing with the sounds that he could see and manipulate. She left him anyway. As did his second wife. She didn't last as long as the first. He told himself he didn't care. He knew he was lying.

ONE CHRISTMAS EVE, twenty-six years after the incident, he wandered alone in a store oblivious to the bustling crowd of shoppers as he watched the crystallized sound above them, crashing into each other. He had no one to buy anything for. He hadn't spoken to his brother in years.

The orchestral version of "Silent Night" began to play in the background, its soft waves like a blue mist drifting over and through the crystallized voices and the song's melody brought tears to his eyes. He'd loved that song as a child.

All is calm, all is bright.

He'd never felt that way. He couldn't be silent. But a part of him missed it. But he didn't dare crave it again. He'd never make another wish. It was too dangerous. This noise was his punishment. If he hadn't made that wish he could have lived with the shouting, then he'd still have a family.

HE RETURNED to his car and pressed a button to turn on the music. But it didn't work. Nothing worked. Silence surrounded him.

A still silence. Like the quiet of a grave.

His heart began to race.

He frantically pushed other buttons, checked connections. Nothing. He grabbed his cell phone, his hands shaking.

"It's no use, it won't work," a tiny voice said.

Damion spun around and saw a woman sitting in the back seat. "What the f—?"

She wagged a finger at him. "No, no, watch your language."

He almost laughed. She was the size of a two year old, but fully formed as an adult, dressed in a red and green outfit and talking to him like his school principal. She had toffee colored skin, silver white hair and big brown eyes. To his annoyance he noticed she was pretty. Before he could speak, she disappeared then appeared in the passenger seat beside him. "I'm sorry I scared you."

He didn't want to admit that he was still scared. She looked harmless, but...she couldn't be real. Where had she come from? How could she appear one moment and disappear the next? Was he hallucinating? "What...what are you?"

She gestured to her hat and tapped on the silver bell. She smelled like peppermint and cinnamon sticks. "Can't you guess?"

He shook his head.

She crossed her legs. "Doesn't matter. At least you didn't say an elf because you'd be right and wrong at the same time."

He didn't even know that was possible. "What?"

"I'm here to help you with your wish."

"I didn't make a wish."

"Of course you did. I wouldn't be here if you didn't."

He gripped the steering wheel. He wasn't a tall man, but next to her he felt like a giant. He wanted her gone. "Fine, I wish my music would work."

"No, that's not it. You want silence."

"No, I don't. I asked for that as a kid."

"Your wish wasn't answered then."

He stroked his beard, pretending not to care. "My parents died."

"That wasn't silence. It was—"

He didn't care. "I'm fine. Get out of my car."

"Then why are you shouting?"

"I always shout. If you don't like it you can leave."

"Unfortunately, I can't. I have to do what I'm told."

"I just told you—"

"Not by you," she said with a solemn shake of her head, "but somebody else. It's time you started working."

"Working?"

"Yes, we let you wander for a while wondering if

you'd ever figure it out, but you didn't so I'm here to help you."

"Figure it out? Figure what out?" He frowned. "You're not making any sense. I don't know who or what you are but—"

"You may not know who I am, but I know you." She narrowed her pretty eyes and pointed at him. "I know *what* you are."

"I'm human and you're a—"

She shook her head. "You're partially human. Your mother briefly had an affair with one of us." Her face split into a wide, mischievous grin. "Not that I can blame her, Rai is very tempting and likes to cause trouble. Your father never knew about it."

She didn't give him a chance to reply, not that he had anything to say. He stared at her dumbfounded. "The pain ends tonight, "she said before she touched his hand and the world went black.

WHEN HE CAME TO, they stood on the landing of a grand house with large, portrait oil paintings on the walls. He saw a little girl sitting on the top stairs, dressed in a green nightgown with tears in her eyes.

"She can't see us so you don't have to worry," the tiny woman said.

"What are we doing here?"

"Memory cleaners." She handed him an object that looked like a hammer.

"What am I supposed to do with this?"

"Didn't you ever wonder why as a little boy you couldn't achieve silence no matter how hard you tried? How it seemed to feel real to you? It's because you're a sensor. People like you are rare even among our type, but you can see and taste and even touch sound. Tonight we're going to clean this house because the sounds of the former tenants are still in the walls and affecting the people in the house."

Damion felt a sudden rage. "You're telling me all this now!"

"I was there," she said in a soft voice.

"No, you weren't. All this time I've felt like I didn't belong. As if something was wrong with me and you're telling me that I'm not fully human and that I'm suppose to start helping strangers and—"

The tiny woman blinked. "That's good."

"What's good?'

"Your anger. You haven't been really angry in a long time. Use it tonight."

He didn't move. "Why are you coming to me now? Why didn't you come then? Why didn't anyone help us? If it's just the sounds then why didn't a memory cleaner—"

"Your family was too broken. There was nothing we could do."

He dropped the hammer. "Then you can't help her either," he said looking at the girl. "She just needs to grow up and escape. That's what my brother did. I don't want to be here."

The melody "Silent Night" drifted towards him from an unknown source twisting his heart. The hammer appeared back in his hand.

"Prove it," the woman said.

Damion took the hammer and slammed it against the wall. It shattered like glass, revealing another wall behind it. A wall that shimmered with fresh, clean air.

"Good job. That would have taken me much longer."

He stared at the shattered pieces around him and watched them slowly melt into the ground. He looked up and saw that the little girl's tears had dried up. She raced down the stairs and her father greeted her with a hug.

"What happened?" he asked amazed.

"The argument ended with forgiveness," the woman said in a simple, happy tone. "Let's go to the next house."

"But I don't want..."

Seconds later Damion stood in a stylish apartment fitted with white leather seats and abstract metal statues. His companion rested her hands on her tiny hips and shook her head as she stared at a spot on the cream tiled floor.

"Oooh, this is one stubborn fight. It will take awhile to get the stain out." She handed him a brush.

He frowned. "Why are we using tools? Can't you just wave your hand or something?"

She shrugged. "This is the rule."

He glared at her for a long moment. He had no way to leave. He couldn't seem to frighten her no matter how much he shouted. He relented, got down on his knees and scrubbed out the stain. With each stroke he faintly heard the argument (the same one that had lasted more than ten years and was still unresolved) until it was a barely a whisper.

The sound of crying followed. He looked up and saw two women in tears. One was clearly older than the other, but they were both fashionably dressed.

"That happens sometimes," his companion said, "when you remove the anger the pain underneath comes bubbling out. They'll be okay."

Before he could ask who "they" were or what had happened she touched his arm and they disappeared again. That was how they spent the remainder of the night. After the third place he stopped being angry or annoyed and started to whistle a little. Leaving each place fresh and clean made him feel happy. He never thought he could feel that way again. He was truly invisible and it felt right.

They drifted from offices to apartments to homes until they landed in a place that filled him with dread.

Damion frantically looked around the familiar room. "No, I can't be here."

"It's the last stop."

"I don't care," he said, staring out the window of his brother's master bedroom determined not to see what secrets the room might share. "There's nothing wrong here. It's perfect."

He hadn't spoken to his brother in years. The last time they had met they'd had a massive shouting match. He'd felt energized by it. He loved to needle his brother not knowing why his brother didn't like it too. Then one day his brother stopped talking to him. He told himself he didn't care. He knew he was lying.

"You know he needs you."

"He's got a wife and two kids. He's fine." *He has to be fine. I need him to be fine.*

"The walls say different. You know it."

"He always handled things better than I did. I shouldn't have..." Damion felt his throat tighten. He cleared it. "Charlie married a good woman who stuck with him." His brother had been lucky. He found his sister-in-law dull, meek and listless but she'd given his brother a home. A family.

This is what he wanted. He wanted to know that one of them had escaped and was normal.

He didn't want to know that was a lie.

"Your brother misses you."

Damion shook his head, pressing his palms against the window, although he could feel nothing in this alternative state except the power of his emotions. "No, he's better off. They're all better off."

"Your wish didn't kill your parents."

He knew that rationally, but it didn't make a difference. "My brother thinks so."

"Then turn around."

He took a deep breath. "No."

He remembered having dinner with them once, shocked by how quiet the house was. How well behaved the children were. How his sister-in-law winced whenever Damion spoke, because his brother Charlie only spoke in soft modulated tones. He teased him about that, but admired him as well. This peaceful environment had seemed foreign to him.

"Turn around."

Damion gripped his hands into fists because he knew what the woman wanted him to see. That the quiet, the soft words were an illusion. That the tension and unspoken words were inverted shouts. That his brother's kids lived in the same fear they once had, because of Charlie.

He didn't want to see the bubbling rage of Charlie's anger.

"You have to see it," she said.

He knew she was right. He bit his lip, turned and looked at the walls. He saw the pent up screams.

Sweat covered his skin. He knew those screams. He'd felt them too when the nightmares came—the sound of a gunshot, the thud of a body hitting the ground, the sound of sirens, of racing footsteps.

Soon the nightmare became real and the sounds attacked him from all sides, nothing could give him solace. He felt as if he would go mad. If his brother could not live in silence and he couldn't live in noise where could they go? Perhaps there was no escape. Maybe his mother had the right idea all along. She'd stopped the shouting.

Charlie always pretended not to care.

They'd both been lying to themselves.

"Do you really want a silent night?" the woman asked him in a sweet, soft voice.

He shook his head not willing to admit that he was afraid.

"You can. You know what's on the other side of this wall. You both can have it now."

He wasn't sure he believed anymore but with all his might he lifted his hammer and struck.

HE STOOD outside staring at his brother's front door. A large wreath hung over the brown door. He didn't know how he'd gotten there, but when he looked around he saw his car in the driveway. He didn't know why he was there. He should have called first. He shouldn't surprise them. If his brother saw him now, they'd fight like always and that would be the end of it.

He took a step back. He'd talk to him in the New Year.

The door opened before he could leave. His brother stood there. He registered shock then weariness. They shared the same height and build, but he hadn't sported a beard the last time they'd met and he knew he looked a little rough. Damion took a deep breath and said in a whisper, "I'm sorry, I—"

His brother's eyes filled with tears and he embraced him.

And they cried.

He was sorry for so many things. That their parents' death had separated them, that they'd fought when they'd finally reunited, that he hadn't been there for him. That his shouting was the only way he could love him.

Now a whisper was all he could manage and his brother understood.

When Damion finally stepped inside, he noticed the house felt different. Brighter. The brittle silence that had once clung to its wall had fallen away. His sister-in-law greeted him and looked less small and meek as she once had, the weight of the house no longer dragging her down. "The children are asleep, but—"

"He'll see them in the morning," Charlie said. "We have the guest room ready."

They urged him ahead into the living room then disappeared to get some food in the kitchen. Damion stopped when he saw a young woman standing by the fireplace where a fire quietly burned. When she turned and smiled, his heart stopped.

She smiled and held out her hand. "Hi, my name is Kara."

Damion blinked, unable to trust his eyes, as he took in her red and green outfit, toffee colored skin and silver white hair that matched his. Why did she feel so familiar? "Have we met before?"

She winked at him. "Maybe."

It wasn't possible, was it? Could this be true? This chance?

"I was just going, but your brother has my number if you'd like to get together some time."

He'd like that, but he only nodded. He didn't want to be alone anymore. "You don't have to leave yet."

Her pretty brown eyes held his. "Are you sure?"

He nodded again, realizing he'd never been alone.

That she'd been the woman who'd visited him in his dreams as a child. He was finally truly safe.

Charlie and his wife returned with refreshment. They briefly chatted and ate then settled into a companionable silence. Damion saw the sound of the crackling flames skitter along the ground then he looked up at the decorated tree.

He sighed. His wish had come true. Silence.

Perfect, peaceful silence.

A silent night.

The silence he'd craved before had been broken, his family had been broken, he and his brother had been broken too, but now they could be whole. And with his gift he could help others.

He felt Kara lean into him and she still smelled like peppermint and cinnamon sticks. "Close your eyes," she said.

For the first time in many years, he closed his eyes and smiled.

FOR ALL TIME

FOR ALL TIME

Margery Davis stared at the stack of suitcases and luggage near the front door. There were five of them. All different shapes and sizes but none of them big enough to hold her rage. Not the two black 30-inch packing cases, certainly not the blue duffel bag or the two silver rolling spinners. It wasn't fair that she'd married a liar. A man who only four years ago, on a bright summer's day in front of family and friends had promised to never leave her.

But he had.

Three weeks before Christmas, leaving her with the stain of a memory she'd have to carry with her into the New Year. A memory she could neither drown with tears (she'd tried) or drink away (she'd tried that too). Instead, the memory of Lance left her hollow. She'd kept his things, as a foolish hope that he'd come back. She hadn't been left alone long enough to consider the fact that he might be gone forever. For the past couple weeks she'd been surrounded by friends and family who never arrived empty handed. A refrigerator bursting with food was a testament to that. She had enough frozen jollof rice to last her for months. She could happily stay with her delusion that Lance might return, but it had been the sight of the holiday lights lining the windows and dogwood tree on the yellow colonial across the street that nudged her to move on. It was time she told herself. Time to let go.

Time to forget him.

But she couldn't.

Anger and rage had given her the energy to pack up his things. She'd managed to stuff every last memory of him into the various suitcases—from the green knit sweater his grandmother had made for him, which he'd loved to wear when shoveling them out of a Philadelphia blizzard, to the old watch he'd never gotten around to putting a new battery in. He'd always promised to get to it, but never did. Time was never on his side. Or hers.

She'd waited for a man like him to enter her life. She'd had no intention of getting married. At nearly fifty, she'd been perfectly happy running her consulting business, traveling with friends to the Caribbean and spending time with her nieces and nephews when she got a chance, never imagining that a spilled cup of Americano and a man's sexy laugh would change her life.

She hadn't paid much attention to the tall black man in the maroon blazer who stood ahead of her in line at the coffee shop. And she wouldn't have paid any more attention if she hadn't taken a seat near the window and caught a glimpse of him as he hurried through the parking lot, a strong spring breeze flattening his blazer against his form. She might have turned away if she hadn't seen him place his coffee cup on the top of his silver Mercedes, toss something into the backseat before he jumped in the driver's seat and drive away.

She'd nearly finished her apple cinnamon muffin when he returned. She watched him park his car and enter the coffee shop. He went to the counter again and ordered another cup. She watched him dash out the door and this time before he reached his car he tripped and dropped the coffee, spilling it on the asphalt. He shook his head, scooped up the now empty container and lid and returned to the counter. When he headed towards the exit in the same hurried manner as he had the first two times she couldn't help herself.

"Stop being in such a rush," she told him as if he were one of her nephews although he was much older with grey sprinkled through his black hair.

He turned to her surprised and she waited for him to shoot back a rude reply or ignore her, but instead his brown eyes warmed and then he laughed. The sound was as warm and sweet as the muffin she'd just finished.

"Are you offering lessons?"

"It will cost you a coffee," she said a little surprised by how easy it was to banter with him.

He nodded. "Here. Eleven-thirty tomorrow," he said then left and made it to his car without incident. She only half expected him to show up, but he did. Early.

That was one thing she would find out about him, he

was either running late, or arriving early. It was not something she'd ever managed to change. However, coffee quickly turned to dinner then breakfast. She didn't expect to fall in love with him, but his charming, easy going way seduced her into marriage. He'd been The One for her.

But that hadn't been special enough to make him stay. She'd taken a gamble and lost.

So that cold, brisk December morning she'd dragged the suitcases down the stairs, knocking them against the wooden stairs with a satisfying bang and stacked them near the door ready to call a local charity. But she couldn't take the next step. Ridiculously wishing he would come and do it himself. She'd been foolish to carelessly offer her heart to him. He'd treated her heart as carelessly as he had his coffee. She walked up to the silver suitcase and kicked it. "I wish I'd never met you," she spat out before she turned away.

She walked to the kitchen. A drink. She needed a drink to calm her nerves and then she'd figure out what to do.

She poured herself a large glass of white wine and then another. By the third glass her head began to spin a bit and she rested her head on the table. When she finally felt like herself again and lifted her head, the sun had slipped behind the oak trees behind their house, casting shadows on the table and floor. She wiped her eyes and licked her lips, they tasted salty.

She had been crying. She hadn't remembered that. She rested her head down on her arms and squeezed her eyes shut. How could she have let him hurt her so much? Why hadn't he let her say goodbye? Why had he left her all alone like this? If only she could have one last chance to tell him how much he'd hurt her. To grab him and shake him. She ached all over.

All because she'd trusted him.

"How long are you going to be angry with me?"

Margery froze at the sound of the voice. *His* voice. Her head shot up. She frantically looked around and didn't see anything until she saw a figure come through the dark entryway. No, no. It couldn't be him. This tall black man in a grey sweater and jeans couldn't be...

She scrambled to her feet, shocked and terrified.

"How long?" Lance asked, his voice soft. But his words fell on her ears like boulders. *Time?* He was talking about time at a moment like this? How long? However long it took.

She took another step back, knocking the wooden chair to the ground. It fell with a clatter. "W-what are you doing here?"

His voice sounded sad. "How long, Margery?"

No. No. He had no right to call her name like that. So lovingly, so gentle. Like his warm, brown gaze. He had no right to pretend that he cared.

"You left me," she said her voice barely a whisper. "You have no right to be here."

But of course he did. It was still his house. He could come and go as he pleased. They hadn't divorced. All his things were still there.

"I'll call the police," she said.

"No, you won't."

He was right. The bastard.

She didn't want to see him, didn't want to talk to him. Not sensibly at least.

"Take your things and go!"

She raced up the stairs and buried herself under the covers and squeezed her eyes shut. She kept her body still but her mind raced. She waited to hear footsteps, she knew would never come. She waited to hear the front door open. She waited for a sound she knew she'd never hear again.

"Margery."

"You have no right to be here."

"How long?"

She shoved the bed sheets away and faced him. "As long as I damn well want." She picked up a pillow—his pillow, the one where his scent still lingered—and threw it at him, but it breezed past his head and he didn't flinch.

"I'm getting rid of your things. Do you see that?"

He nodded.

"Why are you here?"

He looked away. "You know it wasn't—"

She rolled her eyes. "Stop." She didn't want to hear his reasons. His excuses: That it wasn't his fault. Life happens, things changed. Love ends.

But that was the worst part. Her love hadn't. It still lingered.

He met her gaze. "Don't be angry with me."

"Why are you here?"

"I couldn't leave things the way they were."

"Yes, you could have. You're free now. Not tied to anyone. Especially not to me. You're in a better place without me. Why are you here now?"

He motioned for her to follow him before he walked out the door. She softly swore then followed him. She found him in the living room standing next to the tall tree in the corner.

The tree.

She'd been foolish enough to buy a Christmas tree.

She'd forgotten about that.

THEIR FIRST TREE together had been a disaster. It had been too big for their house. Their second tree had been a gift from a friend. A silver spruce. Their third had been a beautifully crafted artificial tree that stood nearly eight foot high. Before Lance had left her they'd purchased a real tree. She now knew that had been a mistake. It had been delivered yesterday. The scent of pine filled the house, it stood bare in the corner ready to be dressed in holiday finery—something she and Lance used to do together.

Plus she had to remember to water it.

An artificial tree could be ignored. This tree wouldn't let her. It was still alive, but one day wouldn't be. Like their life together it would end.

She should end it now. "I don't need your help."

He sat on the couch. "You're not hurting anyone, but yourself."

"I don't need a lecture."

Her cell phone alerted her to a text from her sister.

How are you doing?

I'm fine. She replied knowing that was what everyone wanted her to say. They didn't want to worry about her. They didn't want her grief to touch their holiday joy. It had taken all her cunning to get the brief respite of silence she had now.

Need help with the tree?

She looked over at her husband and briefly thought of telling her sister that he was there. That he'd offered to help her. Wasn't that a laugh? But that would only worry her. *No, I'll get to it later. Love you.*

Love you more.

Margery put her phone away and folded her arms. "I'm so angry at you."

Lance stood. "Tell me about it."

And she did. She let all her anger pour forth. She didn't get to shake him, but she did get to shout and cry and rage a little and he listened.

He listened as he carefully strung a series of lights around the tree.

He listened as he hooked ornaments on the different branches.

And he listened as he placed a star on the top of the tree.

Margery sat on the couch and watched him, her voice hoarse, her energy gone. She watched him turn on the switch and the lights burst to life like tiny white candles.

The tree was done. It meant he would be leaving her for good. It was their final time together.

He sat down beside her, close enough to touch, but she felt nothing. "You know love doesn't end when—"

"Don't say it."

"I'll always love you."

"But you still left me." It was too soon, it hurt too much to forgive him even though he'd done nothing wrong.

"I didn't want to go."

This time she believed him. She felt her anger subside. He hadn't wanted to leave her, although he had been forced to. That helped a bit. "I wish I could hold you one last time."

"I know," he said, his voice as tender as a caress. If she closed her eyes, she could imagine the scent of his soap, the touch of his hand. "Can you forgive me?"

The doorbell rang.

She opened her eyes. Her heart filled with dread. She'd learned to dread that sound. The once dulcimer sounds of welcome were now like the warning wail of a fire alarm.

The police had rung the doorbell. They'd walked into her home with their weighted shoulders and cautious gaze to tell her that there had been an accident. They mentioned speed, distraction and no survivors. After their visit the doorbell signified a body to be identified and then buried. Of a new future alone.

If he hadn't been in such a rush... Why was time never on his side?

She turned to see that he was gone.

Again the doorbell had stolen him away.

Margery walked to the front door, pushing his duffel bag to the side with her foot, before she opened it and signed for the package the mail courier handed her. She saw her name written on the label, signed in Lance's handwriting.

He must have sent it before. She returned to the living room, tore open the package and gasped at the sight. Surrounded by blue tissue paper lay a book of photos. Photos of them together. She'd always teased him about taking so many pictures and he told her he wanted to capture every happy moment with her.

Happy. Did she dare let that emotion enter her heart again?

But it did. Joy slowly seeped through the darkness that had gripped her heart as she looked through the surprise gift he'd sent her. Every picture evoked a happy memory of their time together. She slowly went through the book and the pages smelled like him, the touch of the paper warm, as if his hand had touched hers, the sound of each turning page like a whisper of his voice. Pictures of them together and then an inscription: *Always remember how much you are loved.*

Love. That's what she had to remember. His love. Her love. Their love.

Margery closed the book and held it to her chest,

tears filling her eyes. The darkness in her heart melting. She looked at the bare Christmas tree.

There were no string of lights or decorations, but she knew Lance had been there. She still felt his presence and knew he'd given her one final memory. She held the book tighter. This gift was a wish come true. A chance to hold him one last time. She looked down at the cover of the book and saw their smiling faces staring back at her. She saw a woman who loved and was loved. She had taken a gamble, but it had been worth the price.

Can you forgive me? She bit her lip as she thought of the last question.

To this she whispered with a heart filled with promise and love as if she was his bride once more... "I do."

ONE SNOWY NIGHT

ONE SNOWY NIGHT

"Where's Mummy?"

"She'll be back soon."

"When?"

"I don't know."

"Gone so long."

"I know. You mustn't be scared."

"But I'm cold."

Dami was too. She turned to her three year old brother and pulled down his knit cap so that it rested over his ears then secured his scarf a little tighter before she sat back in her seat and rubbed her mittens together.

She tried not to shiver. The inside of the car no longer feeling as welcoming as it had when the heater was on and the sun brightened the dark blue cloth seats.

Now they sat in a cold darkness. The sun had disappeared. Her nose seemed to burn with every breath.

Mum *had* been gone long. She hadn't even said how long she'd be when she left the car in front of the Piggly

Wiggly with a quick "I'm sorry," tossed over her shoulder.

She didn't look at them.

She didn't say why she was sorry or why she'd been crying. It hadn't been dark then. The sun had still been out and there had been lots of cars everywhere. But Dami had been told to stay in the car and now she was too afraid to leave it.

She looked up at the snowflakes swirling, swaying and falling underneath the light of a lamppost a few meters away. A large red ribbon wrapped around it turning it into a silver candy cane.

The snow had already covered the windscreen and made it hard to see ahead of them. Fortunately, the snow hadn't covered the side windows yet. So she stared at the snow and smiled. Perhaps they'd have a white Christmas like she'd read about in books and seen in movies. Then she'd have something to talk about at the new school she'd start in the New Year.

She liked snow. Although she'd been disappointed that it hadn't tasted like sugar as she'd once hoped.

There had been some snow in London but none in Lagos. She barely remembered what it had been like when she left that city at five.

Her mother didn't like snow. She hadn't much liked rain either. She complained about it often. It never rained this much at home she used to say. And her father would sigh and not say anything. Her mother would frown and stare at the doll one of the elders had given her. It was to make her feel less lonely and her mother cared for it and talked to it. At first it seemed to help and then it didn't.

BEFORE THE SNOW, her mother had complained about the sun. The sun was too bright. Too hot.

In Lagos, her mother frequently snapped at the driver for driving too slow or too fast, for the air conditioner not working or working too well. She'd even once argued with a soldier at a checkpoint. It got so bad they were all forced to leave the safety of the car, step out into the blazing hot breath of the sun, and go to another place with more grim faced soldiers who held shiny, black guns. The driver pleaded with her mother not to cause trouble but his pleas only agitated her more.

Dami made sure to stay still and quiet as she sat in one of the plastic chairs a soldier had pointed to. She'd been taught not to cause trouble. She'd been told she'd caused trouble enough.

When her father eventually arrived, Dami could tell he was angry. But he didn't look it. His sharp nose, full lips and dark skin polished like a wooden mask of calm. Her father was a very quiet person and she could barely hear his voice over the raised ones of the soldiers and her mother, but finally they were allowed to leave.

Her father said nothing on the way home.

He said nothing at dinner, letting his favorite, crispy Nigerian fried rice, go cold and hard. The scent of curry and thyme seeming to drift through the room each time he moved the rice around on his plate.

It was after dinner, when Dami was safe in bed, that she heard him shouting. He asked her mother if she had a death wish.

"Do you have a death wish?" he kept repeating. "Do you? Do you? Tell me now if you do."

Dami didn't know why he put such force on those words, but it rang in her mind because he said the words with such rage. She didn't know why her mother wishing someone dead angered her father so much.

Dami knew that wasn't good, certainly not for a Christian, but an Auntie who visited from Canada, often wished her husband and his mistress would drop dead and no one seemed upset about it.

They left Nigeria soon after.

THE SUN WASN'T TOO hot or too bright in London. Instead they arrived during a soggy, sweet spring.

They no longer had a driver and there were no soldiers Dami could see. But they did have a housekeeper.

Mum didn't snap at the housekeeper. Instead she mumbled about the rain. She didn't use to complain about the rain before. But in London the rain was too wet. Too frequent. Too cold.

Her mum didn't work anymore and spent most of her time staring out the window of their new flat. She was supposed to stay home with her, that's what her father had said, but her mother seemed barely there. Longing for sunshine she'd once complained about.

Soon her mother's belly got bigger and bigger. But that didn't change her from muttering about the rain. Muttering that another child wouldn't change anything. Wouldn't make her forget what she'd lost.

She was muttering about the fog and rain when she wet herself. Dami wasn't sure if she should say anything when she first heard the trickle, like a leaking faucet, then saw the puddle of water underneath her mother's multicolored dress. But when the housekeeper saw the sight she cried out in alarm and then Mum was rushed away and the housekeeper stayed overnight, which she never had before. The following day, her mother and father came back with a scrunched faced infant that smelled like baby oil.

Her new brother Paxton, which she thought was a funny name.

It was after her brother joined them that her mother began to forget things.

She forgot them at the tube station. She'd left Dami besides Paxton's pushchair outside the toilets. She came back after what seemed like hours later, looking a little dazed.

She forgot them again outside a Tesco supermarket. Dami had watched her mother drive away then return later.

Dami had been frightened by her mother's new strange behavior, but her father made up for it that

Christmas with a beautifully decorated tree and lots of presents. Dami remembered the scent of cider and the sweet pies she'd enjoyed at a cousin's house. They all sang and laughed.

It was only later when she looked at photos that Dami remembered her mother hadn't been there. That all Christmas Day she hadn't left her room.

She felt a little guilty that she hadn't missed her.

THE SUN and soldiers hadn't driven them away from London. Or the rain and fog. Nothing had. At least nothing seemed to.

Instead, Daddy had gotten a new job. At least that's what an aunt had told Dami, although she'd heard whispers that a change in scene might do well for her mother's health.

But Mum didn't like the snow in South Carolina. The snow was too cold. Too white. She thought the infrequent London snow was better.

But Dami liked snow wherever it fell. She remembered seeing how the sky became a blanket of white over their new three bedroom townhouse with the large evergreen tree out front; how the wind chilled her cheeks. How it didn't fall like rain. She tried to catch it and, sometimes, if she was real still, a snowflake would fall on her mitten and wouldn't melt.

Just lay there glistening in the sunlight.

Her mother complained about the puddles of water

their snow boots left in the mud closet. How the air captured your breath like a spirit.

She'd once heard Auntie Emma say that her mother could find joy nowhere. That she could never recapture the joy lost back home.

Dami wondered too. Her mother seemed to disappear bit by bit, day by day. Melting away like snowflakes caught between two gloves. Something she could see but never grasp. Never keep close.

But Daddy had hoped that Mummy's joy would come back. Daddy always tried to make them all smile in his quiet ways. They were going to get a tree next week and decorate it. This morning Mum had bundled her and Paxton up to go get some decorations. It had been fun at first.

The car had been filled with the bright sound of holiday music, although Mum was still getting used to driving on the wrong side of the road.

Then they were in front of the store. Dami didn't expect to get many holiday decorations at a place called Piggly Wiggly but she liked the name and the shop seemed nice enough.

When the car settled and parked between a big black truck and a tiny green car, Dami began to unlatch her seatbelt, but her mother told her not to. Then she dashed out of the car with the words "I'm sorry."

And Dami still didn't know what her mother had been sorry about.

She meant to ask her.

But she hadn't come back yet.

Had she forgotten them again? Only last week she'd left them in the kid's changing room. Paxton had been getting a new sweater.

Daddy had been so angry. And Mum had cried.

Paxton began to shiver. "I'm hungry."

Dami was hungry too and the cold darkness seemed to bite her fingers and toes. She fought to keep her teeth from chattering. She had to be brave. She had to be obedient.

Even if a part of her didn't want to be.

The snow continued to fall. This time it wasn't silent.

It fell like crushed ice on a glass table and started to cover the white lines on the ground.

She didn't like that the lamplight was too far away so she couldn't see her brother's face. Only hear his voice as an ever increasing darkness swallowed up any lingering shadows.

"When we get home we'll have cocoa and cookies for dinner," she said. "Would you like that?"

She sensed, more than saw, him nod.

He trusted her so she felt a little bad lying to him. There was no way Daddy would let that happen, but if it took Paxton's mind off things it was good. Better than having him crying.

Paxton trusted her so she had to trust Mum. Dami had to trust that she'd come back soon.

But she was beginning to wonder.

She began to wonder if her mother had lied just like she had. She wondered if her mother was really sorry at all.

Dami looked at the snowflakes and felt a chilling feeling of dread. She wondered if she'd ever see her mother again.

STILL.

Her brother had become so still. He wasn't usually like that. He'd swing his foot or bob his head. But right now he didn't move. Dami pulled off a mitten, reached over and touched his chubby, round cheek. It was so cold.

"Paxton?"

"Is Mummy back yet?"

Dami's heart began to pound. His voice sounded so far away even though he was right next to her.

Where was Mum? Why wasn't she back yet? Why had she said she was sorry?

And the snow. The snow was now covering the ground. She saw some car tracks. Heard a car door slam and the crunch of boots and someone rushed inside the store. Maybe she should follow. Maybe she shouldn't listen to what Mum had told her. Maybe she should make her mum angry again. Maybe she should cause a little trouble. It would be better than this.

They had been here so long and they were hungry and cold.

And...

Dami saw someone waving.

At first they seemed in silhouette then slowly came

into focus. A child. Like her. He wore a bright red coat, and black gloves that matched his boots and hat.

She waved back. Glad to see someone smiling when she felt miserable inside.

He motioned her forward.

She shook her head.

He motioned her forward again.

She couldn't leave the car. Could she?

The child came across the parking lot, so swiftly their boots didn't leave any foot prints, and then opened the passenger side door. She hadn't realized Mum hadn't locked it.

He smiled at her.

And she gasped and stared back because she knew him. Because he shared her eyes and smile.

"Let him sleep," the boy said, glancing at Paxton. "Come on. You need to move."

"But Mum—"

"She won't mind."

Dami opened the door and instead of feeling scared she felt free. It had felt colder inside the car than it did outside of it. She took a deep breath, the frosty air seeming to burn her lungs.

Painfully glorious.

And the snow. She could enjoy the snow.

The boy with eyes that mirrored hers spun around and laughed and Dami did the same.

Suddenly bright lights appeared through the blanket of darkness as if thousands of fairy lights had been strung across the night sky.

She told him about their new house and Dad's plans for their Christmas tree. She told him that she missed him.

He told her that he loved her.

And she told him she was sorry. And he kissed her on the cheek and told her there was nothing to be sorry for.

And she let herself believe him.

Kemi wouldn't have gotten sick if Dami hadn't been so strong.

It isn't right for a girl to be so strong.

Quiet she might hear you.

I don't care if she does. She should know her place.

Kemi pulled a face and made Dami laugh and she let the pain of her mother's words fade away. I love you too, she said, and took his hands in hers.

She invited him to visit with them. And he only smiled and Dami knew that he wouldn't come even though she knew Daddy would like to see him.

"Now it's time for you to go," her twin brother told her.

"But—"

"Go inside the shop and call Daddy."

"Mum will get in trouble."

Her brother blinked, patient. The same patient expression he'd had when he'd gotten sick; when he sat in the large hospital bed with a plush, white pillow behind his bald, brown head. He could still smile, while Dami could barely see him through her tears. Mum had been wrong. She wasn't the strong one. He was. He'd always given her courage. She would trust him. "Mum's with me now," Kemi said. "You have to look after Daddy."

Dami knew what he meant. Her mother had been longing for him since his passing. She hadn't hated the sun and the rain before. Perhaps she wouldn't have hated the snow either if she'd seen Kemi like this. Seen how happy it would have made him.

But now her mother was in a place where she didn't have to hate anything, feel anything, long for anything. Just welcome peace.

Her brother sighed. "Don't be angry with her."

Strangely she wasn't. She'd felt she'd lost her mother the day she'd buried her brother.

The pain had been greater because her mother could no longer look at her with love but with longing. Longing for another child. Dami knew she was a poor replacement.

Now she didn't have to be one.

"Go Dami. Be brave. Be strong. Paxton needs you." Kemi squeezed her hands then she felt a whispery soft kiss on her cheek before she found herself inside the dark car again.

She looked out the window and did not see their foot prints in the snow.

A KIND CLERK with a bushy black mustache and hairy knuckles allowed Dami to use his phone.

She dialed with shaking fingers—fear, cold, worry, excitement all mixing together.

"Daddy?" she said when the line connected.

"Where are you?" he said, his voice deep, sharp.

"Please don't be angry."

"I'm not angry," he said, but his voice hadn't lost its sharp edge. The tone that sometimes made Mum cry. Dami felt like crying too.

"Where are you?"

"Inside the Piggly Wiggly," she said. "It's dark." She didn't know why she mentioned that.

"Let me talk to your mum."

"She's...she's not...she's..." Tears choked her words.

"Never mind, my brave girl," he said his voice becoming soft. "Stay where you are. I'll be right there."

Dami bit her lip hoping that was true.

FORTUNATELY, the snow stopped falling and the kind clerk gave them some soft chocolate chip muffins to eat while they waited for their father.

When the front glass doors opened a rush of cold air came in but Dami didn't feel it as her father's face came into view. She didn't remember moving.

But she did remember the feel of his warm, strong embrace. He smelled like coffee, fried cassava and snow.

His body shook and she heard him sniff.

She'd always seen her mother cry, but never her father. His tears felt different. More present, like a wounded animal than like the soft echoing cries of her mother.

"I'm so sorry," he said.

Even his words sounded different than her mother's had. Each word tinged with a quiet, lingering sorrow.

Dami didn't want him to be sad. He was the one always trying to make them happy in his steady, quiet way. And he had.

"Daddy don't cry." Dami patted his back. "I'm here. I'm here."

He pulled away and stared at her then her brother before his gaze shifted back to hers and he smiled.

And her heart lifted because she knew that he didn't need her to be someone else. She couldn't replace Mummy or her twin and he didn't need her to.

One day she'd tell him about Kemi. About how she'd played with him in the snow. How he'd given her the courage to leave the car and call him. That he was always with them and that he didn't have to worry about Mum anymore. That Kemi would look after her.

This holiday they would make memories with Paxton and eat cocoa and cookies and decorate the tree now that the two ghosts were gone: The living one now resting with the one who had gone before her.

Dami saw the love in her father's brown gaze and hugged him again in relief.

She too could rest at last.

She didn't disappoint him. She didn't have to feel guilty for being the one who lived. She didn't have to be afraid to be alive. To live with joy. To giggle with Paxton. To enjoy this holiday season.

Her father once had called her his precious gift.

And at that moment, she felt like it.

But more than that, she felt the gift of his unwavering love.

THE LIST

THE LIST

The old man was struggling.

Lamar watched him as a brisk wind swept through the parking lot, nipping at the collar of his worn bomber jacket. He shoved his hands in his pockets and leaned against the No Parking sign. He wanted to rush over and help, but he kept his distance. He had to plan how he approached the old man in the green and black flannel jacket, who looked like a packed mule as he strained to carry too many grocery bags.

The overcast sky made the day seem later than it actually was, as if it were closer to evening instead of early afternoon. The red ribbons on the utility poles seemed to be the only thing that gave the day any color. Even the large decorative snowflakes seemed to fade under the grey gloom. He heard the chirp of birds and the crinkle of cellophane as a group of birds found treasures inside a discarded bag of potato chips; a woman talking loudly on her phone in a language he couldn't distinguish, while a man in a full beard sat in his truck and wolfed down his lunch as the muted sound of a base beat pounded through the closed windows.

Nobody seemed to notice the old brown skinned man, with hair as grey as the sky, inching his way down the accessibility incline.

But Lamar did.

He adjusted the straps of his backpack before he shoved his hands back in his pockets. He had to approach the old man cautiously and with a smile so that he wouldn't trigger fear. He was used to people looking at him with fear in their eyes. Lamar knew all about fear. Every day of his life he pretended he wasn't afraid, although that was all he ever felt. Soon that'd be over. He wouldn't have to be afraid no more, but first he had to help the old man.

He crossed the parking lot and kept his voice light when he said, "Need a hand?"

The man paused, frowned, looked at him with suspicion. At least it wasn't fear. That was a good sign. Lamar had always been big for his age. At eighteen he just brushed 6'1 and they said he'd likely keep growing. Not that it would matter anyway.

The man seemed to take in Lamar's worn jacket and jeans and black sneakers with no laces, he kept them that way because the shoes were tight and he couldn't afford another pair.

He smiled at the old man. A practiced smile: A slight

curve of the mouth, showing no teeth. It was hard for him to smile, he rarely had anything to smile about, but this man was worth the effort.

It took him only a few seconds to realize that the man hadn't said anything; the old man looked up at him almost frozen. His frown stayed in place but his brown eyes began to fill with tears.

Lamar took a panicked step back. "Whoa, whoa, whoa. I'm just trying to help." He held up his hands in surrender. "I wasn't trying to rob you or nothing."

The old man set his bags down with a tired sigh. "I know that," he said in a full-bodied deep voice that shocked Lamar by its resonance. "It's just—" He wiped his eyes. "Nobody's asked me that and meant it in a really long time."

Up close the man didn't look as fragile as he'd appeared from a distance. He stood average height with a stocky frame. Perhaps it was the bags that had made him look so small only moments before.

Lamar lifted most of the grocery bags leaving two for the old man to carry. "Where's your car?"

He shook his head as if in regret. "No car. I'm taking the bus."

Lamar heard the rumbling of an engine that made his heart sink. He turned to the street and saw a bus pulling away from the curb. "That bus?"

The old man released a laugh. "Yeah."

Lamar set the bags down trying to gauge how quickly he could get to it if he ran fast. "Maybe I can—"

"No, don't try to stop it. I'll wait for the next one." He reached for the bags, but Lamar picked them up before he could. "I'll carry them there. You just take those two, sir." They were the lightest of the group.

"You can call me Mr. Howard."

"Lamar."

"Thank you, Lamar."

For a moment Lamar felt as if the soft, warm touch of a sun beam had broken through the grey clouds. Mr. Howard's words touched his heart, made it feel a little less frozen. He was still cautious, still afraid, but he was helping someone and that felt good.

THERE WAS ONLY one other person at the bus stop: A skinny woman with East African features wearing a peach colored wool coat, typing something on her cell phone. She sat on the bench and had two bulging shopping bags taking up the rest of the space. Lamar cleared his throat. She cut him a disinterested glance and kept typing. He cleared his throat a little louder. She looked up and glared at him.

He glared back. *Don't mess with me, mama. Not today.* He shifted his gaze to the old man then at the crowded bench. She curled her lip but took the hint and removed her bags.

Lamar pointed to the now empty seat and Mr. Howard sat.

"You really bought too much if you were planning to take the bus," Lamar said, shoving his hands in his pockets.

"I forgot I didn't have a car."

Lamar silently swore. Did the old guy have dementia or something?

Mr. Howard's keen gaze caught Lamar's expression and he smiled. "I forgot I let my daughter borrow the car," he clarified.

"Why did you let her borrow your car?"

"Hers is in the shop."

"Then why isn't she riding the bus instead of you?"

The old man grew quiet and Lamar knew he'd said too much. He always said too much. *You ask too many questions. You get on people's nerves,* that's what his fifth foster mother liked to tell him.

He shifted his gaze to the bakery across the street, feeling heat steel into his cheeks, and mumbled, "I'm sorry."

"No, don't be," Mr. Howard said with such force Lamar turned to look at him. "Don't ever apologize for caring. You hear me?"

Lamar nodded not knowing what else to say.

Mr. Howard hung his head and Lamar heard him sniff. The old man was sad. To Lamar sadness was like a scent. He could pick it up anywhere and this man reeked of the raw, numbing sadness that all the holiday cheer couldn't brush away. If he could make him smile, even a little bit, it would be worth it.

"You got a lot of food and stuff here," Lamar said, making his voice light. "I could help you get through it if you didn't want to carry them home."

Mr. Howard rewarded him with a laugh then looked at him for a long moment. So long Lamar got defensive. What was he looking at? What did he see? People rarely looked at him, saw him. He was like a shadow.

"How would you like to earn that privilege?" Mr. Howard finally said.

"Huh?"

"You busy today?"

He hadn't been busy in a long time. Didn't plan to be busy ever again. "No."

"My wife's coming out of the hospital tomorrow and I want to get things ready for her." He pulled out a list from his jean's pocket. "I have a lot to do and could use some help."

"You don't even know me."

"Friends always start out as strangers first."

Friends. He didn't have those. He'd tried but it had never worked out. "Sure, I'll help you."

THE OLD MAN COULD WALK.

It felt like a mile after they got off the bus before they reached the little bungalow tucked inside a maze of a suburban neighborhood. The white and blue house was nice, but when Mr. Howard opened the front door Lamar thought he would hurl. The house stank. He looked around the small living room (where a bouquet of dead flowers marinated in stagnant dirty water), wishing he could cover his nose but both his hands were full so he chose to breathe out his mouth, which made things only marginally better.

Mr. Howard turned to him. "What's wrong?"

"You don't smell that?"

"Sorry," Mr. Howard said with a shrug. "I left a bunch of dishes in the sink, I need to wash them."

"It smells like something died. No offense, but unless your dishes are covered in sewage it ain't them." He went into the kitchen and saw a white garbage bag leaning next to an overflowing trash bin, the sink piled with dishes and crumbs on the kitchen table. He opened up the fridge and saw fruit rotting. He swore.

"You said you have a daughter?" Lamar asked just to make sure.

"Hmm."

He wasn't going to judge. No, he was lying. He *was* going to judge. This daughter of theirs could take her Dad's car but never once stepped inside to see the state of the kitchen? First thing on Mr. Howard's list was to put the food away, but that wasn't going to happen. First, Lamar was going to take out the trash and open all the windows. He was going to clean out the fridge, put the food away and then clean the dishes. He was surprised to find a stack of laundry too when he opened the windows in the living room.

That had also been an item on the list, as well as

changing the bed sheets and replacing the light bulbs in the hallway.

Lamar was up for the challenge.

One thing he was good at was cleaning. At his seventh foster home the house was always tidy. He remembered it smelled fresh like lemons. He liked his foster parents and maybe his foster mother would have kept him if he hadn't discovered she was having an affair with a delivery guy. He'd promised her he wouldn't say anything, but she hadn't believed him.

He had one great foster dad but then he got sick and his wife said she couldn't deal with the cancer and a teenager so Lamar had to go. Lamar was always the first to go, like an unwanted appliance. When you don't belong to anyone you're easy to discard.

He scrubbed the bathroom tub, pleased at the progress he'd made getting through Mr. Howard's list, and briefly wondered if his former foster dad had made it through. He hoped so. Although he knew hope didn't mean much.

He jumped and turned when he felt a tap on his arm. He'd shed his jacket hours ago and had rolled up his sleeves, but Mr. Howard still wore his flannel coat. He wondered if the old man was cold.

"I've got you some food," Mr. Howard said before Lamar could speak. "Come on."

He sat at the small, freshly cleaned, kitchen table and tried not to eat as if he hadn't eaten in days, which was only partially true. He'd survived on a banana and a beef jerky, but trying to tamp down his raging hunger proved hard when he faced the bowl of warm minestrone soup and a roasted chicken sandwich Mr. Howard had just bought from the grocery store.

Mr. Howard watched him in the same probing way he had before but instead of feeling defensive, Lamar felt okay. He was getting used to him.

"You need a haircut."

He grunted. He'd heard that more than once. People always seemed to act like a haircut was something you could get done for free.

"When you're through eating, I'll get my gear."

"You're a barber?"

Mr. Howard stood and left the room, Lamar wasn't sure if he hadn't heard him or was ignoring him. He decided not to care.

He finished his lunch, cleared the table and then turned his chair so that Mr. Howard could start cutting his hair.

Lamar closed his eyes. He couldn't remember the last time someone touched him in any way—whether harshly or tender, absently or with intent. He felt Mr. Howard's hand as he tilted is chin, heard the sound of the scissors. For a moment he could pretend that he mattered. He remembered his first haircut, didn't know how old he was, but he remembered feeling proud by how he'd been praised for being so brave while another kid cried at the sound of the razor. His high pitched screams like those of a wild animal being attacked.

But Lamar reveled in the praise, he wasn't praised much. He made it his mantra to be brave no matter how scared and alone he felt. Be brave.

But right now, in Mr. Howard's newly cleaned kitchen, sitting in a stiff chair getting his hair cut, he didn't have to be anything but be still. If he sat still enough he could stretch out this moment. He could be safe and warm; fed and dry. The streets wouldn't be his home; the fragrance of loneliness soaked in sadness wouldn't follow him.

"Your family is going to be surprised when they see you," Mr. Howard said with pride.

The magic moment burst. Lamar took a moment to answer: Silence let dreams live. Words killed them.

"Don't have a family." He shrugged. "It's okay. I'm used to it."

"What are you doing over the holidays?"

"I've got plans," he said. At least he knew he wasn't lying about that. He didn't like lying to the old man.

Mr. Howard patted him on the shoulder then handed him a black handheld mirror. "Good?"

Lamar didn't look at his new haircut; instead he looked at the reflection of the man smiling behind him. "Yeah."

Mr. Howard's face grew serious. "But I need you to do one thing for me."

Lamar felt his pulse kick up speed. He knew that expression. Mr. Howard's eye's weren't just probing now. They were intense. It meant he'd done something wrong. He swallowed. "What?"

"Stop using a razor. You see those bumps on your neck and cheeks?"

He felt his face burn. He knew he was ugly. "Yeah. I got acne."

"It's not acne. They're razor bumps. The way the razor interacts with the hair on your face and neck disturbs it. Follow me. Let me show you what you need to do."

Mr. Howard took him to his master bathroom, the one with a bright orange shower curtain and fuzzy flower shaped bathmat, and showed him a new way to shave before he said, "In no time those bumps will go away."

"Really?" Lamar said wanting to believe him, but too afraid to hope.

He nodded before he broke into a wide smile. "It was one of the few things my dad taught me, aside from 'stay away from liquor and another man's wife.'" He shook his head and sighed although his brown eyes still twinkled with mischief, "But he didn't always follow his own advice and there were a lot of other things I had to figure out on my own."

Lamar felt himself relax. He'd learned something. Not just about shaving, but about Mr. Howard too. He didn't have the perfect childhood and didn't sugarcoat it. His probing brown eyes told him a multitude more than words ever could.

Yeah, he knew all about having to figure things out on his own. He didn't have any stories about his dad to share. He'd never had anyone teach him how to shave.

Food, clothing, shelter and school. Those were the basics and every place he stayed at gave him those things, to varying degrees, but there were the little details about life that no one prepared him for. Puberty had been a bitch. His balls dropped but his voice didn't for years. A big guy with a soft voice—sheer hell. Then, when his voice finally did drop, it came with no warning. One day he sounded like he'd swallowed helium, the next like he'd swallowed a cave. It freaked him out. Freaked his foster parents out too. His foster mother literally screamed when he'd said "Good morning" to her while she made breakfast.

It hadn't been a good day.

But he didn't have a lot of good days. Soon that'd be over.

But today was good. Today was nice. Today he wasn't afraid of anything. "What's next on the list?"

Holiday decorations.

Lamar had never seen an attic with so much stuff. When he helped Mr. Howard decorate the Christmas tree, he feared it would topple under the weight of all the ornaments—some store bought, some handmade—but Mr. Howard was determined to put up as many as could fit. They also set candles in the windows and decorated the couch with three red and white holiday pillows that said: Believe, Peace, Joy.

Lamar was tying a red balloon to one of the standing lamps in the living room when the front door flew open and a loud voice said, "I brought back the car, Dad. But I didn't get a chance to put gas in it." She saw him then froze. "Who the hell are you?"

The moment Lamar saw Mr. Howard's daughter he knew he'd never like this woman with her long fake lashes and faux fur coat. She looked exactly like the pictures of her Mr. Howard had around the house. She looked cute when she was about five years old, smiling in a pumpkin patch, she didn't look cute about forty years later. There was a drawn, hungry look to her narrow features.

"This is my friend Lamar," Mr. Howard said.

Her eyes narrowed with suspicion. Not fear. A win for him. He could deal with suspicion.

"A friend huh? Where did you meet?"

"In the parking lot at the local grocery store."

Lamar stifled a groan. He saw the daughter's eyes shift from suspicion to disgust. She reminded him he was homeless and probably looked it. "Well, you can leave now," she said.

Mr. Howard shook his head. "We're not finished yet."

"Dad—"

"Your mother's coming home tomorrow and I want the place to look nice."

"But Dad you—"

"I know what I'm doing."

His daughter pulled at his sleeve, but he yanked his arm away. She lowered her voice, "Dad, you cannot invite some strange guy into your house—"

"That's enough."

"And not know anything about him." She sent Lamar a look. "He could be—"

"I said enough!" His voice boomed with such force it stunned Lamar and the balloon popped in his hands. He swore. They'd only managed to find three in an almost empty packet in the attic. Mr. Howard had wanted to use them to welcome his wife home, now, because of him, there'd only be two. He was usually so careful. He'd given Mr. Howard another reason to be angry and that was the last thing he wanted to do.

He saw his great day ending. He felt sadness mingling with the fissures of fear he'd allowed himself to briefly forget. He'd better leave now before he was told to go. He'd gotten tired of being told he had to leave. He began to mutter an apology, but when he looked at Mr. Howard's face the words caught in his throat.

Mr. Howard was staring at his daughter in a way that made the old man, again, not seem so old anymore or even as fragile as before. It was as if anger had given him new life, filled him with a towering fire. Lamar didn't dare move, afraid to have any of that fire directed at him.

"You have no right to come in here," Mr. Howard

said, his voice no longer loud, but just as powerful. "He is my friend. In less than twenty four hours he's made up for thirty years of friendships and fifty years of raising you." He lifted his hand when she opened her mouth. "You remember when you told me to go on one of those social media sites you were always on about? You told me it was a way to connect with my friends, to be less isolated, that I had to move with the times. Well, I did. I signed up and chatted, and connected with some old friends and made some new ones, and I told them about your mother and how hard it's been for me and they asked me what they could do. So I…"

He paused and took a deep breath. "…I told them. It wasn't easy for me to do. Asking for help is hard for me, but I did because they were my friends and I needed them. I gave them a list of things that they could do for me. That same list you've been too busy to help me get through." He bit his lip. When he spoke again his voice shook. "And no one replied. Not one single person.

"I wouldn't have made it through this day without this young man. Lamar came over to me and asked if I needed help. He didn't ask for anything in return. That is what I consider a true friend. At this moment he is my friend. So you can take your useless, empty words and leave us to prepare for your mother's return. I'm going to the kitchen now to get Lamar and myself something to drink, when I return I expect you gone." He left.

Lamar still didn't move; the remnants of the ruined balloon clenched in his fist.

Mr. Howard's daughter tugged on the collar of her

coat clearly upset. "He's not usually like that. He's just overly tired. I know he didn't mean a word he said."

Lamar knew he should nod but was afraid to. He still didn't like her but he felt a little sorry for her. Mr. Howard's words had been harsh, but he wondered if they'd also been true.

"I would have helped out more, but I was busy—*am* busy. They're cutting jobs left and right at my company and at my age I know they're ready to replace me with someone younger. I wasn't staying away because I wanted to. I love my parents."

Again Lamar didn't nod, but this time not because he was afraid, but because he was angry. Her words sounded hollow. If she loved her parents so much why hadn't she filled the car with gas? Helped clean the dishes? Gotten holiday decorations from the attic? She still didn't hear the sadness in her father's voice; understand how much he needed her.

He felt angry that she had parents and he didn't. But life wasn't fair. She had a mother who was sick but alive. A father who was old. His parents didn't get to be old.

He didn't plan to get old either.

Her eyes swept the room, careful not to look at him. "You've done a good job here. Better than I could, so I guess, I'll just leave you to it." Her cell phone alerted her to a text and when she read the message her pinched features relaxed a fraction. "That's my ride." She raised her voice. "Bye Dad! See you later." She turned and walked out the front door.

Mr. Howard returned to the living room with two

cups of warm cider. He and Lamar sat on the couch and sipped it in silence for a few moments before Mr. Howard said, "Deep down she's a good woman. We spoiled her. That's our fault not hers."

Lamar shrugged. It was none of his business but his anger and envy grew. Mr Howard's daughter could get a second, third, a hundredth chance in life. She could mess up and make mistakes and she had parents who would forgive her no matter what because they loved her. Nobody had ever loved him like that. No one ever would.

Mr. Howard pulled out the list and studied it.

Lamar sipped his cider hopeful. "Is there anything else?"

"No, that's it."

He felt his hopes shrivel and die. He hated to hear that. He hated that he couldn't be of use anymore. He didn't have a license so he couldn't say he'd drive Mr. Howard to the hospital. But he didn't want to be useless. An idea came to him. "I'm sorry about the balloon. I could go to the store and get—"

"I lied," Mr. Howard said in a quiet voice, cutting through Lamar's words. "When I posted this list online, one person did reply. They sent me flowers and a basket of fruit I didn't need, but once they were here I couldn't throw them away."

Lamar thought of the dead flowers and the rotting fruit and understood. In his backpack he still had an old action figure he should have thrown away years ago but hadn't because it had been given to him by his first friend in kindergarten, a girl with bucked teeth who liked to make the sound of different car engines (her father had been a mechanic).

Lamar stood. He liked Mr. Howard but he was getting too attached. It was time to go.

He grabbed his backpack, which rested against the coffee table. He frowned. It felt different. Lighter. He opened it and frantically checked inside. He knew what was missing.

He heard the sound of Mr. Howard pulling out something from the pocket of his flannel coat. He'd wondered why Mr. Howard had kept his coat on, but now wondered how long he'd known Lamar's secret. "Looking for this?" Mr. Howard said.

His heart raced. He didn't raise his head. He knew what would be in Mr. Howard's hand—a gun. "It's for protection," he lied.

"From other people or from life?"

He wasn't in the mood for riddles. He needed to leave. He wouldn't be afraid. He had to be strong one last time. He straightened and faced the old man, trying to look as fierce as he could. "It's none of your business."

"No, but I care."

"I didn't ask for that."

"I saw you have a list too."

He froze.

Anger. Exposure. Betrayal.

He raised his voice. "You shouldn't touch someone else's stuff."

"I found it on the ground."

"You're lying."

Mr. Howard slowly rose to his feet. "Yes, I am. Just like you are. But I've been doing it a lot longer and few things frighten me anymore."

Lamar felt his mouth grow dry as he faced Mr. Howard's dark, unwavering gaze. This old man was not as old as he thought; the grey of his hair suddenly reminding Lamar of storm clouds rather than a simple overcast day. This was a man of power, insight. He wasn't what he'd first seemed to be.

"You're not just a retired barber, are you?"

"Is that *really* what you want to ask me?"

No, but he was afraid. Mr. Howard held the gun like a professional, but he hadn't spotted any military or police paraphernalia around the house. Who was this man?

He'd been around firearms before. He still didn't look at Lamar with fear. Shouldn't a black kid with a gun inspire that? At least some unease or suspicion, right? Instead, Mr. Howard looked...worried.

Lamar felt his heart ache. He didn't need anyone worrying about him now. He had plans. He held out his hand. "I've gotta go."

"Tell me about your list."

He gripped his hand into a fist.

"I told you about mine."

Lamar shook his head, fighting tears.

Mr. Howard looked down at the lined, crumpled white sheet of paper. "Looks like you've got most of the things crossed off. Number one: Write to your uncle."

Yeah, he'd had an uncle he vaguely remembered. He was serving time on a drug charge. He'd gotten caught selling marijuana before the drug was made legal; his family just had shitty luck.

"Give Juan your comics."

When Lamar had briefly lived with Juan's family it was the one thing they could talk about.

Mr. Howard mumbled as he quickly read through the rest of the list before he fell silent and looked up at him. "Looks like there's a lot you're giving away."

He shrugged. "It's the holidays." And he'd already done it. He didn't need them anymore.

So many others his age had life figured out. One girl who'd aged out of the foster care system already had a job lined up, another had a family supporting him going to college, and another was living with his girlfriend's parents.

He had nothing. There was no future for him.

Mr. Howard looked down at the gun. "So what was the plan? A bullet to the head or death by cop?"

Lamar held his gaze. He'd thought about a bullet to the head. He knew the exact location in the woods he'd planned to do it. But death by cop would be easier. Swift. Quick. They wouldn't shoot to wound, they'd shoot to kill and then it would be over.

But just for a brief moment he'd be seen, he'd be a threat, but at least someone would see him—he'd matter. He didn't even know why he'd been born.

He glanced at the gun then back at Mr. Howard's face. "It's for protection." He held out his hand again, ready to take the gun back.

"I took out the bullets."

Lamar swore but he wouldn't argue. No point fighting him. Fighting meant he cared. He couldn't let himself care about anything. Not anymore. He needed to leave the brightly colored holiday lights and decorated tree. He needed to leave the warmth coming from the kitchen and the scent of spiced cider. He needed to leave Mr. Howard so that he could be there for his wife. He turned to the door. "I should go."

"Why? You're already home."

Lamar spun around so fast he nearly lost his balance. What was he saying? His heart pounded. Did he really hear right? Had he imagined it?

"What should we have for dinner?"

Lamar stared at him barely able to form words. "B-but...you don't want me."

Mr. Howard held his gaze. "Yes, I do."

"But I'm—"

"I don't care."

Damn he was crying and he didn't want to cry. But he couldn't seem to get the tears to stop. Hot streaks fell down his face. He covered his eyes.

He felt Mr. Howard's hand on his shoulder and he cried some more.

He didn't have to leave. He could stay. He had a place to stay.

He shook his head, afraid to believe it. "You don't mean it."

Mr. Howard squeezed his shoulder, his voice full of emotion. "I do. You can stay here as long as you like."

"But your wife—"

"While you were cleaning the bathroom, I called her and let her know. She's looking forward to meeting you."

He was still afraid to completely believe him, but he allowed hope to shine through a little, even if he could get a week or two and not be on the streets, that'd be something.

"I have a couple of other things around the house I could use help with in exchange. Does that sound like a fair trade?"

Lamar shook his head.

"You want money instead?"

He shook his head again.

Mr. Howard frowned. "What is it then?"

Lamar looked at a picture of Mr. Howard's daughter hanging on the wall and knew exactly what he wanted. He wanted a picture there too. One day he wanted to earn the honor to be like a son to him. But he couldn't say the words. Was too shy to. "Nothing."

Mr. Howard patted him on the arm, tears touching his eyes. "You're right. Never mind what I said. The only thing friends need to exchange is trust."

Lamar nodded feeling the tension within ebb. He knew Mr. Howard would understand.

He resisted the urge to hug him, his heart buoyant. He had a friend, someone who thought he mattered. Someone who mattered to him. He felt like he belonged in this world. He turned to the door.

"Where are you going?" Mr. Howard called after him.

"To get more balloons, I saw a store—"

Mr. Howard grabbed his car keys from off of the side

table. "We can get them together then pick up something for dinner to eat when we come back home."

Home.

Lamar opened the front door and inhaled the crisp cold air and couldn't stop a smile.

Finally. At last. At last.

He had a home.

ABOUT THE AUTHOR

Dara Girard, an award-winning, national bestselling author of more than forty novels and many short stories, from romance to suspense, loves telling stories.

Born in the US to immigrant parents, Dara enjoys pulling from her Jamaican, British, Nigerian heritage and exposure to various cultures to bring what reviewers and fans call "vivid emotional stories" to life. She is best known for her popular Henson Series, the mysterious Clifton Sisters, and the fun Black Stockings Society.

Visit her website to sign up for her newsletter and get sneak peeks, monthly updates on new releases, and special offers.

For more information visit
www.daragirard.com